ACCORDING TO JEEVES

Titles by P. G. Wodehouse

Jeeves and Wooster

The Inimitable Jeeves
Carry On, Jeeves
Very Good, Jeeves
Thank You, Jeeves
Right Ho, Jeeves
The Code of the Woosters
Joy in the Morning
The Mating Season
Ring for Jeeves
Jeeves and the Feudal Spirit
Jeeves in the Offing
Stiff Upper Lip, Jeeves
Much Obliged, Jeeves
Aunts Aren't Gentlemen

Blandings Castle

Something Fresh
Leave it to Psmith
Summer Lightning
Full Moon
Pigs Have Wings
A Pelican at Blandings
Sunset at Blandings

Uncle Fred

Uncle Fred in the Springtime
Cocktail Time
Service with a Smile

Monty Bodkin

The Luck of the Bodkins

Standalone novels

The Pothunters
Piccadilly Jim
A Damsel in Distress
The Adventures of Sally
The Small Bachelor
Money for Nothing
Big Money
Hot Water
Laughing Gas
Summer Moonshine
The Girl in Blue

ACCORDING TO JEEVES

THE WIT AND WISDOM OF

P. G. Wodehouse

HUTCHINSON
HEINEMANN

1 3 5 7 9 10 8 6 4 2

Hutchinson Heinemann
One, Embassy Gardens
8 Viaduct Gardens
Nine Elms
London SW11 7BW

Hutchinson Heinemann is part of the Penguin Random House group of companies whose addresses can be found at global.penguinrandomhouse.com.

This collection © The Trustees of the Wodehouse Estate, 2024
All quoted material copyright © P. G. Wodehouse with the exception of the quotation from Lady Ethel Wodehouse on p. xii, taken from *The World of P. G. Wodehouse* by Herbert Warren Wind, published by Hutchinson in 1981.
Introduction © Alan Titchmarsh, 2024

The Trustees of the Wodehouse Estate have asserted
P. G. Wodehouse's right under the Copyright, Designs and
Patents Act, 1988, to be identified as the author of this work

Please be aware that the material included in this book was originally published between the 1910s and 1970s and contains language, themes or characterisations which you may find outdated.

This collection first published by Hutchinson Heinemann in 2024

www.penguin.co.uk

A CIP catalogue record for this book is available from the British Library.

ISBN 9781529154146

Set in 11.75/14pt Garamond MT
Typeset by Falcon Oast Graphic Art Ltd
Printed and bound by [to be supplied by production]

The authorised representative in the EEA is Penguin Random House Ireland, Morrison Chambers, 32 Nassau Street, Dublin D02 YH68.

Penguin Random House is committed to a sustainable future for our business, our readers and our planet. This book is made from Forest Stewardship Council® certified paper.

www.greenpenguin.co.uk

MIX
Paper | Supporting responsible forestry
FSC® C018179

Penguin Random House is committed to a sustainable future for our business, our readers and our planet. This book is made from Forest Stewardship Council® certified paper.

Contents

Introduction	ix
Jeeves on Family	1
Jeeves on Love and Romance	7
Jeeves on Food and Drink	23
Jeeves on Fashion	31
Jeeves on Appearance	37
Jeeves on Animals	45
Jeeves on Nature	55
Jeeves on Shakespeare	61
Jeeves on Literature	67
Jeeves on Philosophy	87
Jeeves on Mishaps	99
Jeeves on Health	113
Jeeves on Law and Order	117
Jeeves in Translation	123
Jeeves on the English Language	133
Jeeves on Bertie	139
Jeeves on Other People	145
Jeeves on Jeeves	155
Editor's Note	157

Introduction

Reginald Jeeves is the one exception to the rule that 'nobody loves a smart-arse', even though he himself, when commenting on such a situation to his 'gentleman' Bertram Wooster, would couch his opinion more felicitously:

'Might I venture to suggest, sir, that a person who gives the impression of omniscience is most likely to be treated by society with some degree of opprobrium.'

I forgive Jeeves his air of superiority because of his finely crafted phraseology and the fact that his endeavours are almost always directed at salvaging the disastrous situations unwittingly wrought by his hapless employer.

This paragon of valeting virtue sprang from the pen of the man who I, and many others, consider to be the finest comic writer this country has ever produced. Granted, 'comic' might seem to suggest a thinness of style, but the style of Pelham Grenville Wodehouse (known as 'Plum' since his childhood) is anything but thin. There are many, myself included, who simply cannot get enough of him and his various characterful creations, be they billeted at Blandings Castle in

Shropshire, or Berkeley Mansions in Mayfair. Aside from the Wodehouse style and the literary craftsmanship, the very nature of the books – their Edwardian otherworldliness – makes them volumes into which one can dive when the tawdriness of dystopian drama and the darkness of Scandi-noir begin to pall. That literary titan Evelyn Waugh opined that 'Mr Wodehouse's idyllic world can never stale . . . He has made a world for us to live in and delight in.' In the words of Bertie Wooster, I consider that 'E.W. has hit the n on the h.'

I confess to aspiring to become Clarence, ninth Earl of Emsworth, in my dotage – not for the elegance of the title, but for the ability to live contentedly, deep in the British countryside, under a clear blue sky, scratching the back of my prize-winning pig while birds sing and bees buzz in the flowerbeds of my Arcadian demesne. While not wishing to confine my reading matter to that of Augustus Whiffle, whose porcine knowledge is clearly of unimpeachable repute, I do concur with Cicero that 'If you have a garden and a library, you have everything you need.' It is a sentiment that I hope might receive an approving nod from Jeeves, though we are not apprised of any horticultural acuity on his behalf. His pronouncements on nature tend to be of a poetic turn of phrase: 'There is a fog, sir. If you will recollect, we are now in autumn – a season of mists and mellow fruitfulness.' However, he was clearly well acquainted with certain aspects of natural history, for when Bertie suggests that 'You must have heard of newts. Those little sort of lizard things that charge about in ponds,' Jeeves replies: 'Oh, yes, sir. The aquatic members of the family *Salamandridae* which constitute the genus *molge*.' (It would be idle to deny that there are times when Jeeves does not shy away from showing off.)

Bertie, while not unaffected by the caprices of the weather or the beauty of the countryside, is undoubtedly happiest at his club – the Drones – in the company of such characters as Bingo Little, Gussie Fink-Nottle and Pongo Twistleton, whose predilection for hurling bread rolls would, had their membership been that of the Athenaeum, have been greeted by the Edwardian clergy of that establishment with a disdainful snort and hasty expulsion.

Among all these personages, whose names are like those of old friends to me and countless other Wodehouse addicts, Reginald Jeeves is, perhaps, the most resonant. His Christian name is never used by his employer. His surname – which universally has come to represent that of the archetypal gentleman's gentleman – has a touching history. It was first used by Wodehouse in a short story published in 1916: 'Extricating Young Gussie'. The already established writer (his first book, *The Pothunters*, had been published in 1902) saw the first-class cricketer Percy Jeeves play for Warwickshire against Gloucestershire in 1913. That Percy died in the Battle of the Somme three years later, at the age of just twenty-eight – the year in which that short story was published – gives the choice of name a certain poignancy.

From the authentic tone of his books, one might assume that Wodehouse was accustomed to being surrounded by a host of domestic staff, and for one short period in his life, that much was true. In 1928, in his late forties, he and his wife Ethel owned two houses: one in Le Touquet, France, and the other in Norfolk Street, London. The English home possessed 'a butler, a footman, a cook, a scullery maid, two housemaids, a parlour maid and a chauffeur who drove the Rolls-Royce'. For most of their married life, in Remsenburg, Long Island, they employed a couple who looked after the household, but Mrs Wodehouse did admit that prior to this 'we had only one really exceptional servant. He was a butler named Kreutz – an Austrian – who was with us the year we lived in southern France. He had worked in embassies most of his life, because he had a naturally dignified manner and spoke half a dozen languages. Kreutz was a very, very nice man – nothing at all like those pompous butlers in my husband's books.'

But then, Jeeves was not a butler. He was a valet – even though, when push came to shove, he could, according to Bertie, 'buttle with the best of them'. But for most of the time he was a general factotum, a companion, a facilitator and an all-round good egg. He and Bertram Wilberforce Wooster appeared in thirty-five short stories and eleven full-length novels, the first of these being *Thank You, Jeeves* in 1934 and the last *Aunts Aren't Gentlemen* in 1974.

Throughout these books, we come to know a widely read, self-reliant individual whose knowledge of literature is clearly a reflection of the man from whose pen he sprang. Whereas Bertie frequents the Drones, Jeeves joins his fellow valets and butlers at the Junior Ganymede Club, whose club book (now running to twelve volumes) contains information about the employers of the members and, as such, is a record of considerable sensitivity. The members play bridge and, clearly in the case of Jeeves, spend much time reading. While Bertie relies heavily upon his childhood familiarity with the Old Testament, which resulted in his winning the scripture prize at school – hence his tendency to repeatedly compare his ordeals at the hands of such tyrants as Roderick Spode with those of Daniel in the lion's den – Jeeves evinces a wider understanding of world literature: the classics, Latin aphorisms, Greek myths and the works of Shakespeare. But his real forte is poetry, and he will, at the drop of Bertie's reviled Tyrolean hat, quote Keats, Shelley, Longfellow, Burns, Rossetti, Tennyson, Wordsworth and Pope. He is fond of referring to the philosophers Schopenhauer and Spinoza but finds Nietzsche 'fundamentally unsound'.

Aside from his literary knowledge – and worldly wisdom – the one thing that makes Jeeves's discourse so enjoyable is his syntax. He is not so much verbose as apposite and elegant in his mode of expression. One has the feeling that his conversation is crafted to amuse himself as much as to impress Bertie, over whose head it regularly takes flight. It is a way of channelling his exasperation, which might otherwise result in a degree of inadvisable candour. Not that he always seeks to disguise his prejudices when offering advice: 'I would hesitate to recommend as a life's companion a young lady with quite such a vivid shade of red hair. Red hair, sir, in my opinion, is dangerous.'

Of one thing the reader can be certain: when Jeeves puts his foot down, it stays down. He is a man of unwavering opinion – in lesser mortals it might be described as a 'stubborn streak' – but whether it is a lack of appreciation for his master's modest accomplishments on the banjolele, or for a particular item of clothing to which Bertie seems especially attached and which is abhorrent to his valet, we know that in the end Jeeves will triumph and that any self-congratulation on his part will be undertaken silently, with perhaps the merest hint of a smile.

It is highly likely that few of us could, in reality, live with Jeeves and his arch omnipresence, but it is absolutely certain that without him Bertie Wooster would be lost – and our bookshelves would be all the poorer.

Alan Titchmarsh, 2024

Jeeves on Family

JEEVES SPEAKING TO BERTIE

'I have had little or no experience with children.'

'Fixing it for Freddie', *Carry On, Jeeves*

BERTIE SPEAKING TO JEEVES

'Jeeves, I wish I had a daughter. I wonder what the procedure is?'

'Marriage is, I believe, considered the preliminary step, sir.'

'Bertie Changes His Mind', *Carry On, Jeeves*

JEEVES SPEAKING TO BERTIE

'An invalid undoubtedly exercises a powerful appeal to the motherliness which exists in every woman's heart, sir.'

'The Spot of Art', *Very Good, Jeeves*

JEEVES SPEAKING TO BERTIE

'It is a recognised fact, sir, that there is nothing that so satisfactorily unites individuals who have been so unfortunate as to quarrel amongst themselves as a strong mutual dislike for some definite person. In my own family, if I may give a homely illustration, it was a generally accepted axiom that in times of domestic disagreement it was necessary only to invite my Aunt Annie for a visit to heal all breaches between the other members of the household. In the mutual animosity excited by Aunt Annie, those who had become estranged were reconciled almost immediately.'

Chapter 23, *Right Ho, Jeeves*

BERTIE SPEAKING TO JEEVES

'What's that thing of Shakespeare's about someone having an eye like Mother's?'

'An eye like Mars, to threaten and command, is possibly the quotation for which you are groping, sir.'

Chapter 8, *The Mating Season*

Jeeves on Love and Romance

JEEVES SPEAKING TO BERTIE

'You consider total abstinence a handicap to a gentleman who wishes to make a proposal of marriage, sir?'

Chapter 13, *Right Ho, Jeeves*

JEEVES SPEAKING TO BERTIE

'One must remember, however, that it is not unusual to find gentlemen of a certain age yielding to what might be described as a sentimental urge.'

'Indian Summer of an Uncle', *Very Good, Jeeves*

BERTIE REMINISCING

I remember Jeeves saying on one occasion – I forget how the subject had arisen – he may simply have thrown the observation out, as he does sometimes, for me to take or leave – that hell hath no fury like a woman scorned. And until tonight I had always felt that there was a lot in it.

Chapter 23, *Right Ho, Jeeves*

'Until [Lord Chuffnell's] financial status is sufficiently sound to justify him in doing so, his self-respect will not permit him to propose marriage to the young lady.'

'Silly ass!'

'I would not have ventured to employ precisely that term myself, sir, but I confess that I regard his lordship's attitude as somewhat hyper-quixotic.'

'Development of Butter Situation', *Thank You, Jeeves*

BERTIE SPEAKING TO JEEVES

'What would a girl say, Jeeves, who, having had a row with the bird she was practically engaged to because he told her she looked like a Pekingese in her new hat, wanted to extend the olive branch?'

'"So sorry I was cross", sir, would, I fancy, be the expression.'

'The Ordeal of Young Tuppy', *Very Good, Jeeves*

JEEVES SPEAKING TO BERTIE

'Physical exercise is a recognised palliative when the heart is aching, sir.'

'Development of Butter Situation', *Thank You, Jeeves*

JEEVES SPEAKING TO BERTIE

'Mr Sipperley has this moment gone, sir,' he said, as I came charging out.

I halted and mopped the brow.

'Jeeves,' I said, 'what has been happening?'

'As far as Mr Sipperley's romance is concerned, sir, all, I am happy to report, is well. He and Miss Moon have arrived at a satisfactory settlement.'

> 'The Inferiority Complex of Old Sippy',
> *Very Good, Jeeves*

BERTIE SPEAKING TO JEEVES

'And the engagement's off?'

'Yes, sir. The affection which her ladyship felt for Sir Roderick was instantaneously swept away on the tidal wave of injured mother love.'

'Development of Butter Situation', *Thank You, Jeeves*

JEEVES SPEAKING TO BERTIE

'It merely crossed my mind, sir, that for a gentleman of your description Miss Wickham is not a suitable mate [. . .] In my opinion Miss Wickham lacks seriousness, sir. She is too volatile and frivolous.'

'Jeeves and the Yule-Tide Spirit', *Very Good, Jeeves*

JEEVES SPEAKING TO BERTIE

'[Wives] are generally open to suggestions from the outside public with regard to the improvement of their husbands, sir.'

'Jeeves and the Old School Chum', *Very Good, Jeeves*

JEEVES SPEAKING TO BERTIE

'Gentlemen who have been discarded by one young lady are often apt to attach themselves without delay to another, sir. It is what is known as a gesture.'

Chapter 18, *Right Ho, Jeeves*

JEEVES COMMENTING TO BERTIE ON LORD
CHUFFNELL'S FEELINGS FOR PAULINE STOKER

'I am, of course, aware that his lordship is experiencing for the young lady a sentiment deeper and warmer than that of ordinary friendship, sir.'

Chapter 5, *Thank You, Jeeves*

JEEVES SPEAKING TO BERTIE

'I am on terms of some intimacy with the elder Mr Little's cook, sir. In fact, there is an understanding.'

I'm bound to say that this gave me a bit of a start. Somehow I'd never thought of Jeeves going in for that sort of thing.

'Do you mean you're engaged?'

'It may be said to amount to that, sir.'

'Well, well!'

'She is a remarkably excellent cook, sir.'

'Jeeves Exerts the Old Cerebellum',
The Inimitable Jeeves

BERTIE SPEAKING TO JEEVES

'Girls of high and haughty spirit need kidding along. This cannot be done by calling them carrot-topped Jezebels.'

'No, sir.'

'I know if anyone called me a carrot-topped Jezebel, umbrage is the first thing I'd take. Who was Jezebel, by the way? The name seems familiar, but I can't place her.'

'A character in the Old Testament, sir. A queen of Israel.'

'Of course, yes. Be forgetting my own name next. Eaten by dogs, wasn't she?'

'Yes, sir.'

Chapter 11, *Jeeves in the Offing*

Jeeves on Food and Drink

JEEVES SPEAKING TO BERTIE

'If you would drink this, sir,' he said, with a kind of bedside manner, rather like the royal doctor shooting the bracer into the sick prince. 'It is a little preparation of my own invention. It is the Worcester Sauce that gives it its colour. The raw egg makes it nutritious. The red pepper gives it its bite. Gentlemen have told me they have found it extremely invigorating after a late evening.'

'Jeeves Takes Charge', *Carry On, Jeeves*

JEEVES SPEAKING TO BERTIE

'One cannot make an omelette without breaking eggs, sir.'

I started.

'Omelette! Do you think you could get me one?'

'Certainly, sir.'

'Together with half a bot. of something?'

                              Chapter 23, *Right Ho, Jeeves*

BERTIE SPEAKING TO JEEVES

'You have the air of one about to make a remark, Jeeves.'

'Oh, no, sir. I note that you are in possession of Mr Fink-Nottle's orange juice. I was merely about to observe that in my opinion it would be injudicious to add spirit to it.'

'That is a remark, Jeeves, and it is precisely –'

'Because I have already attended to the matter, sir.'

Chapter 16, *Right Ho, Jeeves*

BERTIE SPEAKING TO JEEVES

'Yes, we got together in the hall at, I suppose, about one a.m. I had gone down to see if I could get a bit of that steak and kidney pie.'

'I quite understand, sir. It was an injudicious thing to do, if I may say so, but the claims of steak and kidney pie are of course paramount.'

Chapter 10, *Stiff Upper Lip, Jeeves*

JEEVES SPEAKING TO BERTIE

'I understand that Miss Bassett has recently been reading the life of the poet Shelley, sir, and has become converted to his view that the consumption of flesh foods is unspiritual. The poet Shelley held strong opinions on this subject.'

Chapter 7, *Stiff Upper Lip, Jeeves*

'Medical research has established that the ideal diet is one in which animal and vegetable foods are balanced. A strict vegetarian diet is not recommended by the majority of doctors, as it lacks sufficient protein and in particular does not contain the protein which is built up of the amino acids required by the body. Competent observers have traced some cases of mental disorder to this shortage.'

Chapter 7, *Stiff Upper Lip, Jeeves*

JEEVES SPEAKING TO BERTIE

'A gentleman mellowed by a good dinner is always more amenable to overtures of any kind than one who is waiting for his food.'

Chapter 14, *Aunts Aren't Gentlemen*

Jeeves on Fashion

BERTIE SPEAKING TO JEEVES

'Lots of fellows have asked me who my tailor is.'
'Doubtless in order to avoid him, sir.'

'Jeeves Takes Charge', *Carry On, Jeeves*

JEEVES SPEAKING TO BERTIE

'Pardon me, sir, are you proposing to appear in those garments in public?'
[...]
'You think them on the bright side?'
'Yes, sir.'
'A little vivid, they strike you as?'
'Yes, sir.'
'Well, I think highly of them, Jeeves,' I said firmly.

'Jeeves and the Kid Clementina', *Very Good, Jeeves*

BERTIE SPEAKING TO JEEVES

'There are moments, Jeeves, when one asks oneself, "Do trousers matter?"'
'The mood will pass, sir.'

Chapter 5, *The Code of the Woosters*

BERTIE SPEAKING TO JEEVES

'What do ties matter, Jeeves, at a time like this?'
[. . .] 'There is no time, sir, at which ties do not matter.'

'Jeeves and the Impending Doom', *Very Good, Jeeves*

Jeeves on Appearance

JEEVES SPEAKING TO BERTIE

'Perhaps the young gentleman will not notice that you have a face like a fish, sir.'

'Episode of the Dog McIntosh', *Very Good, Jeeves*

JEEVES SPEAKING TO BERTIE

'It seemed to me that Mr Glossop's face was sicklied o'er with the pale cast of thought.'

Chapter 13, *Right Ho, Jeeves*

JEEVES SPEAKING TO BERTIE

'I would always hesitate to recommend as a life's companion a young lady with quite such a vivid shade of red hair. Red hair, sir, in my opinion, is dangerous.'

'Jeeves and the Yule-Tide Spirit', *Very Good, Jeeves*

JEEVES TO MR BLUMENFELD, SR

'One of Mr Wooster's peculiarities is that he does not like the sight of gentlemen of full habit, sir. They seem to infuriate him.'

'You mean, fat men?'

'Episode of the Dog McIntosh', *Very Good, Jeeves*

'The gentleman who came to the flat wore horn-rimmed spectacles, sir.'

'And looked like something on a slab?'

'Possibly there was a certain suggestion of the piscine, sir.'

Chapter 1, *Right Ho, Jeeves*

'Was Nobby alone?'

'No, sir. There was a gentleman with her, who spoke as if he were acquainted with you. Miss Hopwood addressed him as Stilton.'

'Big chap?'

'Noticeably well developed, sir.'

'With a head like a pumpkin?'

'Yes, sir. There was a certain resemblance to the vegetable.'

Chapter 1, *Joy in the Morning*

JEEVES SPEAKING TO BERTIE

'Sir?'

'It's no good saying "Sir?" You know perfectly well what I mean. Entirely through your instrumentality, I shall shortly be telling Uncle Percy things about himself which will do something to his knotted and combined locks which at the moment has slipped my memory.'

'Make his knotted and combined locks to part and each particular hair to stand on end like quills upon the fretful porpentine, sir.'

Chapter 20, *Joy in the Morning*

Jeeves on Animals

BERTIE SPEAKING TO JEEVES

'Newts, Jeeves. Mr Fink-Nottle has a strong newt complex. You must have heard of newts. Those little sort of lizard things that charge about in ponds.'

'Oh, yes, sir. The aquatic members of the family *Salamandridae* which constitute the genus *molge*.'

Chapter 1, *Right Ho, Jeeves*

BERTIE SPEAKING TO JEEVES

'This is the end of a perfect day, Jeeves. What's that thing of yours about larks?'

'Sir?'

'And, I rather think, snails.'

'Oh, yes, sir. "The year's at the spring, the day's at the morn, morning's at seven, the hillside's dew-pearled —"'

'But the larks, Jeeves? The snails? I'm pretty sure larks and snails entered into it.'

'I am coming to the larks and snails, sir. "The lark's on the wing, the snail's on the thorn —"'

'Now you're talking. And the tab line?'

'"God's in His heaven, all's right with the world."'

Chapter 14, *The Code of the Woosters*

BERTIE SPEAKING TO JEEVES

'Cat? What cat?'

'The one you met at Eggesford Court, with which the horse Potato Chip formed such a durable friendship. Miss Cook was urging Mr Porter to purloin it.'

'Golly!'

'Yes, sir. The female of the species is more deadly than the male.'

Chapter 9, *Aunts Aren't Gentlemen*

BERTIE SPEAKING TO JEEVES

'Suppose the dog won't come away with me? You know how meagre his intelligence is. By this time, especially when he's got used to a new place, he may have forgotten me completely and will look on me as a perfect stranger.'

'I had thought of that, sir. The most judicious move will be for you to sprinkle your trousers with aniseed.'

'Aniseed?'

'Yes, sir. It is extensively used in the dog-stealing industry.'

'Episode of the Dog McIntosh', *Very Good, Jeeves*

BERTIE SPEAKING TO JEEVES

'Who was the chap who was always beefing about losing gazelles?'

'The poet Moore, sir. He complained that he had never nursed a dear gazelle, to glad him with its soft black eye, but when it came to know him well and love him, it was sure to die.'

Chapter 11, *Joy in the Morning*

BERTIE SPEAKING TO JEEVES

'I don't want a watchdog to keep me out of my rooms.'

'No, sir.'

'Well, what am I to do?'

'No doubt in time the animal will learn to discriminate, sir. He will learn to distinguish your peculiar scent.'

'Jeeves and the Unbidden Guest', *Carry On, Jeeves*

BERTIE SPEAKING TO JEEVES

'You are letting your attention wander.'
'I beg your pardon, sir. I was observing the dog. If you notice, sir, he has commenced to eat the sofa cushion.'

Chapter 4, *The Mating Season*

BERTIE SPEAKING TO JEEVES

'I recollect you saying [Mr Sipperley] was letting – what was it? – letting something do something. Cats entered into it, if I am not mistaken.'

'Letting "I dare not" wait upon "I would", sir.'

'That's right. But how about the cats?'

'Like the poor cat i' the adage, sir.'

'Exactly. It beats me how you think up these things.'

Chapter 1, *Right Ho, Jeeves*

JEEVES SPEAKING TO CAPTAIN BIGGAR

'Poorly informed as I am on the subject of the larger fauna of the East, I do not believe that rhinoceri are equipped with licence numbers.'

Chapter 8, *Ring for Jeeves*

Jeeves on Nature

JEEVES SPEAKING TO BERTIE

'There is a fog, sir. If you will recollect, we are now in autumn – season of mists and mellow fruitfulness.'

Chapter 1, *The Code of the Woosters*

JEEVES SPEAKING TO BERTIE

'The stars, sir.'

'Stars?'

'Yes, sir.'

'What about them?'

'I was merely directing your attention to them, sir. Look how the floor of heaven is thick inlaid with patines of bright gold.'

'Jeeves—'

'There's not the smallest orb which thou beholdest, sir, but in his motion like an angel sings, still quiring to the young-eyed cherubims.'

'Jeeves—'

'Such harmony is in immortal souls. But whilst this muddy vesture of decay doth grossly close it in, we cannot hear it.'

Chapter 14, *Joy in the Morning*

JEEVES SPEAKING TO BERTIE

'Full many a glorious morning have I seen flatter the mountain tops with sovereign eye, kissing with golden face the meadows green, gilding pale streams with heavenly alchemy. Anon permit the basest clouds to ride with ugly rack on his celestial face and from the forlorn world his visage hide, stealing unseen to west with this disgrace.'

Chapter 1, *Much Obliged, Jeeves*

BERTIE RECALLING TO GUSSIE FINK-NOTTLE A COMMENT FROM A RECENT EVENING

'I met [Jeeves] airing the dog in the park one evening, and he said, "Now fades the glimmering landscape on the sight, sir, and all the air a solemn stillness holds."'

Chapter 9, *Right Ho, Jeeves*

Jeeves on Shakespeare

BOKO FITTLEWORTH SPEAKING TO JEEVES

'What did Shakespeare say about ingratitude?'

' "Blow, blow, thou winter wind," sir, "thou art not so unkind as man's ingratitude." He also alludes to the quality as "thou marble-hearted fiend".'

Chapter 15, *Joy in the Morning*

JEEVES SPEAKING TO BERTIE

'I have been giving the matter some thought, and am now in a position to say "Eureka!"'

'Say what?'

'Eureka, sir. Like Archimedes.'

'Did he say Eureka? I thought it was Shakespeare.'

Chapter 13, *The Code of the Woosters*

JEEVES SPEAKING TO BERTIE

'Who steals my purse steals trash; 'tis something, nothing; 'twas mine, 'tis his, and has been slave to thousands. But he who filches from me my good name robs me of that which not enriches him and makes me poor indeed.'

'Neat, that. Your own?'

'No sir. Shakespeare's.'

Chapter 5, *Much Obliged, Jeeves*

BERTIE SPEAKING TO JEEVES

'I don't blame [Aunt Dahlia] for being jumpy. She's all tied up with an enterprise of pith and something.'

'Of great pith and moment, sir.'

'That's right.'

'Let us hope that its current will not turn awry and lose the name of action.'

'Don't you mean "agley"?'

'No, sir.'

'Then it isn't the poet Burns?'

'No, sir. The words appear in Shakespeare's *Hamlet*.'

Chapter 12, *Much Obliged, Jeeves*

Jeeves on Literature

BERTIE SPEAKING TO JEEVES

'Who was that pal of yours you were speaking about the other day whose strength was as the strength of ten?'

'A gentleman of the name of Galahad, sir. You err, however, in supposing him to have been a personal friend. He was the subject of a poem by the late Alfred, Lord Tennyson.'

Chapter 11, *Jeeves and the Feudal Spirit*

JEEVES SPEAKING TO BERTIE

'The poet Shelley regarded the matter from the humanitarian standpoint rather than that of bodily health. He held that we should show reverence for other life forms, and it is his views that Miss Bassett has absorbed.'

Chapter 7, *Stiff Upper Lip, Jeeves*

JEEVES SPEAKING TO BERTIE

'I mistrust these elaborate schemes. One cannot depend on them. As the poet Burns says, the best laid plans of mice and men gang aft agley.'

Chapter 15, *Jeeves in the Offing*

JEEVES SPEAKING TO BERTIE

'And we must always remember what the poet Longfellow said, sir.'

'What was that?'

'Something attempted, something done, has earned a night's repose.'

Chapter 21, *Jeeves in the Offing*

JEEVES SPEAKING TO BERTIE

'The poet Tennyson speaks of the little rift within the lute, that by and by will make the music mute and ever widening slowly silence all.'

Chapter 4, *Stiff Upper Lip, Jeeves*

BERTIE SPEAKING TO JEEVES

'I'm glad to be home. What was it the fellow said about home?'

'If your allusion is to the American poet John Howard Payne, sir, he compared it to its advantage with pleasures and palaces. He called it sweet and said there was no place like it.'

'Jeeves and the Greasy Bird', *Plum Pie*

BERTIE SPEAKING TO JEEVES

'Jeeves,' I recollect saying, on returning to the apartment, 'who was the fellow who on looking at something felt like somebody looking at something? I learned the passage at school, but it has escaped me.'

'I fancy the individual you have in mind, sir, is the poet Keats, who compared his emotions on first reading Chapman's Homer to those of stout Cortez when with eagle eyes he stared at the Pacific.'

'Jeeves Gives Notice', *Thank You, Jeeves*

BERTIE AS NARRATOR

I looked at [Aunt Dahlia] with a wild surmise, silent upon a peak in Darien. Not my own. One of Jeeves's things.

'Jeeves Makes an Omelette', *A Few Quick Ones*

JEEVES SPEAKING TO BERTIE

'And thus the native hue of resolution is sicklied o'er with the pale cast of thought, and enterprises of great pitch and moment in this regard their currents turn awry and lose the name of action.'

'Exactly. You take the words out of my mouth.'

Chapter 2, *The Code of the Woosters*

JEEVES SPEAKING TO BERTIE

'Mr Fink-Nottle was commenting to me on the sunset yesterday evening. He said it looked so like a slice of underdone beef that it tortured him to see it. One can appreciate his feelings.'

'I dare say, but I wish he'd keep them to himself. He also appears to have spoken disrespectfully of the Blessed Damozel. Who's the Blessed Damozel, Jeeves? I don't seem to have heard of her.'

'The heroine of a poem by the late Dante Gabriel Rossetti, sir. She leaned out from the gold bar of heaven.'

'Yes, I gathered that. That much was specified.'

'Her eyes were deeper than the depths of waters stilled at even. She had three lilies in her hand, and the stars in her hair were seven.'

Chapter 13, *Stiff Upper Lip, Jeeves*

JEEVES SPEAKING TO BERTIE

'It is the custom at election time, sir. Custom reconciles us to everything, a wise man once said.'

'Shakespeare?'

'Burke, sir. You will find the apothegm in his *On the Sublime and Beautiful*. I think the electors, conditioned by many years of canvassing, would be disappointed if nobody called on them.'

Chapter 8, *Much Obliged, Jeeves*

JEEVES SPEAKING TO BERTIE

'By different methods different men excel.'
'Burke?'
'Charles Churchill, sir, a poet who flourished in the eighteenth century. The words occur in his Epistle to William Hogarth.'

Chapter 8, *Much Obliged, Jeeves*

BERTIE SPEAKING TO JEEVES

'How quiet everything seems now.'

'Yes, sir. Silence like a poultice comes to heal the blows of sound.'

'Shakespeare?'

'No, sir. The American author Oliver Wendell Holmes. His poem, "The Organ Grinders". An aunt of mine used to read it to me as a child.'

Chapter 12, *Much Obliged, Jeeves*

BERTIE SPEAKING TO JEEVES

'What is it the poet says, Jeeves?'

'The poet Burns, sir?'

'Not the poet Burns. Some other poet. About doing good by stealth.'

'"These little acts of unremembered kindness", sir?'

'Indian Summer of an Uncle', *Very Good, Jeeves*

BERTIE SPEAKING TO JEEVES

'I'm like those Light Brigade fellows. You remember how matters stood with them?'

'Very vividly, sir. Theirs not to reason why, theirs but to do or die.'

'Jeeves Makes an Omelette', *A Few Quick Ones*

BERTIE SPEAKING TO JEEVES

'It reminded me of those lines in the poem – "See how the little how-does-it-go tum tumty tiddly push." Perhaps you remember the passage?'

' "Alas, regardless of their fate, the little victims play", sir.'

Chapter 4, *Joy in the Morning*

JEEVES SPEAKING TO BERTIE

'Feminine psychology is admittedly odd, sir. The poet Pope . . .'

'Never mind about the poet Pope, Jeeves.'

'Start Smearing, Jeeves!', *Thank You, Jeeves*

BERTIE SPEAKING TO JEEVES ABOUT GOING TO A BALL

'Why, dash it, I'd rather go to this binge as the meanest Pierrot. Still, I suppose my bally preferences don't count.'

'I fear not, sir. For know, rash youth – if you will pardon me, sir – the expression is Mr Bernard Shaw's, not my own . . . For know, rash youth, that in this star crost world Fate drives us all to find our chiefest good in what we can, and not in what we would.'

Chapter 25, *Joy in the Morning*

Jeeves on Philosophy

JEEVES SPEAKING TO BERTIE

'You would not enjoy Nietzsche, sir. He is fundamentally unsound.'

'Jeeves Takes Charge', *Carry On, Jeeves*

BERTIE SPEAKING TO JEEVES

'Jeeves,' I said, 'have you ever pondered on Life?'
'From time to time, sir, in my leisure moments.'

'Jeeves and the Impending Doom', *Very Good, Jeeves*

JEEVES SPEAKING TO BERTIE

'I wonder if I might call your attention to an observation of the Emperor Marcus Aurelius. He said: "Does aught befall you? It is good. It is part of the destiny of the Universe ordained for you from the beginning. All that befalls you is part of the great web."'

Chapter 4, *The Mating Season*

BERTIE SPEAKING TO JEEVES

'I'm lonely, Jeeves.'
'You have a great many friends, sir.'
'What's the good of friends?'
'Emerson,' I reminded him, 'says a friend may well be reckoned the masterpiece of Nature, sir.'

'Bertie Changes His Mind', *Carry On, Jeeves*

BERTIE SPEAKING TO JEEVES

'It is just possible that an inspiration might pop up. Inspirations do, don't they? All in a flash, as it were?'

'Yes, sir. The mathematician Archimedes is related to have discovered the principle of displacement quite suddenly one morning, while in his bath.'

Chapter 5, *The Code of the Woosters*

JEEVES SPEAKING TO BERTIE AND AUNT DAHLIA WHO ARE TOGETHER

'In affairs of this description, madam, the first essential is to study the psychology of the individual.'

'The what of the individual?'

'The psychology, madam.'

'He means the psychology,' I said. 'And by psychology, Jeeves, you imply—?'

'The natures and dispositions of the principals in the matter, sir.'

'You mean, what they're like?'

'Precisely, sir.'

'Jeeves and the Song of Songs', *Very Good, Jeeves*

BERTIE SPEAKING TO JEEVES

'Yes,' I said. 'Yes, there he is, Jeeves – and, as you say, stooping. But do you really advise—'

'I do, sir.'

'What, now?'

'Yes, sir. There is a tide in the affairs of men which, taken at the flood, leads on to fortune. Omitted, all the voyage of their life is bound in shallows and in miseries.'

Chapter 21, *Joy in the Morning*

BERTIE SPEAKING TO JEEVES

'Then just bust the window, would you mind.'

'I have already done so, sir.'

'You have? Well, you were right about it being noiseless. I didn't hear a sound. Then Ho for the dining room, I suppose. No sense in dillying, or, for the matter of that, dallying.'

'No, sir. If it were done when 'tis done, then 'twere well it were done quickly,' he said, and I remember thinking how neatly he puts these things.

'Jeeves Makes an Omelette', *A Few Quick Ones*

BERTIE SPEAKING TO JEEVES

'There's an expression on the tip of my tongue which seems to me to sum the whole thing up. Or, rather, when I say an expression, I mean a saying. A wheeze. A gag. What, I believe, is called a saw. Something about Joy doing something.'

'Joy cometh in the morning, sir?'

Chapter 1, *Joy in the Morning*

JEEVES SPEAKING TO BERTIE

'Travel is highly educational, sir.'

Chapter 1, *The Code of the Woosters*

Jeeves on Mishaps

BERTIE SPEAKING TO JEEVES

'What's to be done, Jeeves?'
    'We must think, sir.'
    'You think. I haven't the machinery.'
            'Without the Option', *Carry On, Jeeves*

BERTIE SPEAKING TO JEEVES

'Aunt Agatha sent word by Purvis just now that she wanted to see me. Probably she's polishing up her hatchet at this very moment.'

'It might be the most judicious plan not to meet her, sir.'

'But how can I help it?'

'There is a good, stout water pipe running down the wall immediately outside this window, sir. And I could have the two-seater waiting outside the park gates in twenty minutes.'

'Jeeves and the Impending Doom', *Very Good, Jeeves*

BERTIE SPEAKING TO JEEVES

'You agree with me that the situation is a lulu?'

'Certainly a somewhat sharp crisis in your affairs would appear to have been precipitated, sir.'

Chapter 2, *The Code of the Woosters*

JEEVES SPEAKING TO BERTIE

'I was wondering whether in these circumstances you might not consider it advisable to take an immediate departure down the water-pipe. I understand there is an excellent milk-train at two fifty-four. Her ladyship is expressing a desire to see you, sir.'

Chapter 27, *The Mating Season*

BERTIE SPEAKING TO JEEVES

'Jeeves,' I said, 'you will doubtless be surprised to learn that something in the nature of a hitch has occurred.'

'Not at all, sir.'

'No?'

No, sir. In matters where Miss Wickham is involved, I am, if I may take the liberty of saying so, always on the alert for hitches.'

'Jeeves and the Kid Clementina', *Very Good, Jeeves*

JEEVES SPEAKING TO BERTIE

'A broken window would lend greater verisimilitude.'

'Wouldn't it rouse the house?'

'No, sir, it can be done quite noiselessly by smearing treacle on a sheet of brown paper, attaching the paper to the pane and striking it a sharp blow with the fist. This is the recognised method in vogue in the burgling industry.'

'Jeeves Makes an Omelette', *A Few Quick Ones*

JEEVES SPEAKING TO BERTIE

'Mrs Gregson wishes you to call upon her immediately, sir.'

'She does, eh? What do you advise, Jeeves?'

'I think a trip abroad might prove enjoyable, sir.'

I shook my head. 'She'd come after me.'

'Not if you went far enough afield, sir. There are excellent boats leaving every Wednesday and Saturday for New York.'

'Sir Roderick Comes to Lunch', *The Inimitable Jeeves*

JEEVES SPEAKING TO BERTIE

'I had been thinking a good deal about the most suitable method of inducing [Lord Pershore] to abandon his mode of living, sir. His lordship was a little over-excited at the time, and I fancy that he mistook me for a friend of his. At any rate, when I took the liberty of wagering him fifty dollars that he would not punch a passing policeman in the eye, he accepted the bet very cordially and won it.'

'Jeeves and the Unbidden Guest', *Carry On, Jeeves*

'There is no terror, Aunt Dahlia, in your threats, for... how does it go, Jeeves?'

'For you are armed so strong in honesty, sir, that they pass by you like the idle wind, which you respect not.'

'Jeeves Makes an Omelette', *A Few Quick Ones*

JEEVES SPEAKING TO BERTIE

'She is my niece, sir. If I might make the suggestion, sir, I should not jerk the steering wheel with quite such suddenness. We very nearly collided with that omnibus.'

'The Rummy Affair of Old Biffy', *Carry On, Jeeves*

JEEVES SPEAKING TO BERTIE

'I gathered that [Orlo Porter] was under the impression that he was addressing you, and emotion interfered with the clarity of his diction. I informed him of my identity, and he moderated his verbal speed. I was thus enabled to follow him. He gave me several messages to give to you.'

'Messages?'

'Yes, sir, embodying what he proposed to do to you when next you met. His remarks were in the main of a crudely surgical nature, and many of the plans he outlined would be extremely difficult to put into practice. His threat, for instance, to pull off your head and make you swallow it.'

Chapter 14, *Aunts Aren't Gentlemen*

JEEVES SPEAKING TO BERTIE

'It might be advisable if you were to conceal yourself while I conduct the negotiations. Behind the piano suggests itself as a suitable locale.'

'Jeeves and the Greasy Bird', *Plum Pie*

Jeeves on Health

JEEVES SPEAKING TO BERTIE

'Many doctors, I understand, advocate such abstinence [from smoking and drinking] as the secret of health. They say it promotes a freer circulation of the blood and insures the arteries against premature hardening.'

'Jeeves and the Impending Doom', *Very Good, Jeeves*

BERTIE NARRATING

I forget how the subject arose, but I remember Jeeves once saying that sleep knits up the ravelled sleave of care. Balm of hurt minds, he described it as. The idea being, I took it, that if things are getting sticky, they tend to seem less glutinous after you've had your eight hours.

Chapter 6, *Jeeves in the Offing*

JEEVES SPEAKING TO BERTIE

'[Damask is] an archaic adjective, sir. I fancy it is intended to signify a healthy complexion.'

'Bertie Takes Things in Hand', *Thank You, Jeeves*

Jeeves on Law and Order

JEEVES ADDRESSING LADY MALVERN, WITH BERTIE IN ATTENDANCE

'Surely, your ladyship,' said Jeeves, 'it is more reasonable to suppose that a gentleman of his lordship's character went to prison of his own volition than that he committed some breach of the law which necessitated his arrest?'

'Jeeves and the Unbidden Guest', *Carry On, Jeeves*

JEEVES SPEAKING TO MR STOKER, WHO IS AMERICAN

'England is an extremely law-abiding country, sir, and offences which might pass unnoticed in your own land are prosecuted here with the greatest rigour. My knowledge of legal *minutiae* is, I regret to say, slight, so I cannot asseverate with perfect confidence that this detention of Mr Wooster would have ranked as an act in contravention of the criminal code, and, as such, liable to punishment with penal servitude, but undoubtedly, had I not intervened, the young gentleman would have been in a position to bring a civil action and mulct you in very substantial damages. So, acting, as I say, in your best interests, sir, I released Mr Wooster.'

'Black Work in a Study', *Thank You, Jeeves*

JEEVES SPEAKING TO BERTIE

'One does not send gentlemen to prison if one is betrothed to their aunts.'

Chapter 14, *The Code of the Woosters*

BERTIE SPEAKING TO JEEVES

'But how did Gussie get out of stir?'

'The magistrate decided on second thoughts to substitute a fine for the prison sentence, sir.'

'What made him do that?'

'Possibly the reflection that the quality of mercy is not strained, sir.'

Chapter 8, *The Mating Season*

Jeeves in Translation

BERTIE SPEAKING TO JEEVES

'Have you noticed, by the way, how frightfully lax everything's getting now? In Queen Victoria's day a girl would never have dreamed of mentioning livers in mixed company.'

'Very true, sir. *Tempora mutantur, nos et mutamur in illis.*'

Chapter 14, *Aunts Aren't Gentlemen*

JEEVES SPEAKING TO BERTIE

'What I am endeavouring to say, sir, is that I am sorry, but, I am afraid I must enter an unequivocal *nolle prosequi*.'

Chapter 13, *Right Ho, Jeeves*

JEEVES SPEAKING TO BERTIE

'*Carpe diem*, the Roman poet Horace advised. The English poet Herrick expressed the same sentiment when he suggested that we should gather rosebuds while we may. Your elbow is in the butter, sir.'

Chapter 1, *Much Obliged, Jeeves*

BERTIE SPEAKING TO JEEVES

'Spode has got a black eye, which one hopes is painful. In short, on every side one sees happy endings popping up out of traps. A pity that Bingley is flourishing like a green what-is-it, but one can't have everything.'

'No, sir. *Medio de fonte leporum surgit amari aliquid in ipsis floribus angat.*'

'I don't think I quite followed you there, Jeeves.'

'I was quoting from the Roman poet Lucretius, sir. A rough translation would be "From the heart of this fountain of delights wells up some bitter taste to choke them even among the flowers".'

'Who did you say wrote that?'

'Lucretius, sir, 99–55 BC.'

Chapter 17, *Much Obliged, Jeeves*

'Your broad-minded view is to be applauded, sir.'

'One must always strive to put oneself in the other fellow's place and remember . . . remember what?'

'*Tout comprendre c'est tout pardonner.*'

'Thank you, Jeeves.'

Chapter 5, *Aunts Aren't Gentlemen*

JEEVES SPEAKING TO BERTIE

'Possibly the plan I suggested might be considered open to that criticism, sir, but *faute de mieux* –'

'I don't get you, Jeeves.'

'A French expression, sir, signifying "for want of anything better".'

Chapter 9, *Right Ho, Jeeves*

JEEVES SPEAKING TO BERTIE

'You feel that Miss Angela's strictures should not be taken too much *au pied de la lettre*, sir?'
'Eh?'
'In English, we should say "literally".'

Chapter 13, *Right Ho, Jeeves*

'Precisely, sir. *Rem acu tetigisti.*'

'*Rem*—?'

'*Acu tetigisti*, sir. A Latin expression. Literally, it means "You have touched the matter with a needle", but a more idiomatic rendering would be—'

'Put my finger on the nub?'

'Exactly, sir.'

Chapter 4, *Joy in the Morning*

Jeeves on the English Language

JEEVES SPEAKING TO BERTIE

'A telegram, sir,' said Jeeves, re-entering the presence.

'Open it, Jeeves, and read contents. Who is it from?'

'It is unsigned, sir.'

'You mean there's no name at the end of it?'

'That is precisely what I was endeavouring to convey, sir.'

'Jeeves and the Impending Doom', *Very Good, Jeeves*

BERTIE SPEAKING TO JEEVES

'What is it that policies have?'
'I think the word for which you are groping, sir, may possibly be cornerstone.'

Chapter 14, *Aunts Aren't Gentlemen*

BERTIE SPEAKING TO JEEVES

'What are those things circumstances have, Jeeves?' I said.

'Sir?'

'You know what I mean. You talk of a something of circumstances which leads to something. Cats enter into it, if I'm not wrong.'

'Would concatenation be the word you are seeking?'

Chapter 7, *Aunts Aren't Gentlemen*

BERTIE SPEAKING TO JEEVES

'I wouldn't have thought Porter would have shown such what-is-it.'

'Would pusillanimity be the word for which you are groping, sir?'

Chapter 9, *Aunts Aren't Gentlemen*

Jeeves on Bertie

JEEVES SPEAKING TO A MISS TOMLINSON

'I fear I am possibly taking a liberty, madam,' I began, 'but I am hoping that you will allow me to say a word with respect to my employer. I fancy I am correct in supposing that Mr Wooster did not tell you a great deal about himself?'

'He told me nothing about himself, except that he was a friend of Professor Mainwaring.'

'He did not inform you, then, that he was *the* Mr Wooster?'

'*The* Mr Wooster?'

'Bertram Wooster, madam.'

'Bertie Changes His Mind', *Carry On, Jeeves*

JEEVES SPEAKING TO PAULINE STOKER

'I doubt whether the union would have been a successful one. Mr Wooster is an agreeable young gentleman, but I would describe him as essentially one of Nature's bachelors.'

    'Black Work in a Study', *Thank You, Jeeves*

JEEVES SPEAKING TO A TEMPORARY
REPLACEMENT JUST BEFORE HE WENT ON
HOLIDAY

'You will find Mr Wooster,' he was saying to the substitute chappie, 'an exceedingly pleasant and amiable young gentleman, but not intelligent. By no means intelligent. Mentally he is negligible – quite negligible.'

'The Pride of the Woosters is Wounded',
The Inimitable Jeeves

JEEVES'S ADVICE TO BERTIE AFTER HE HAD BEEN KNOCKED OUT OF A DRONES CLUB GOLF COMPETITION IN THE FIRST ROUND

'Possibly you omitted to keep your eye on the ball with sufficient assiduity, sir?'

'Jeeves and the Kid Clementina', *Very Good, Jeeves*

Jeeves on Other People

JEEVES SPEAKING TO BERTIE

'As his lordship's pageboy, Harold does not mix with the village lads.'

'Bit of a snob, what?'

'He is somewhat acutely alive to the existence of class distinctions, sir.'

'The Purity of the Turf', *The Inimitable Jeeves*

JEEVES SPEAKING TO BERTIE

'I think that both you and Lady Florence overestimated the danger of people being offended at being mentioned in Sir Willoughby's Recollections. It has been my experience, sir, that the normal person enjoys seeing his or her name in print, irrespective of what is said about them.'

'Jeeves Takes Charge', *Carry On, Jeeves*

JEEVES SPEAKING TO BERTIE

'I am taking the liberty of regarding His Grace in the light of an at present – if I may say so – useless property, which is capable of being developed.'

'Jeeves and the Hard-Boiled Egg', *Carry On, Jeeves*

JEEVES SPEAKING TO BERTIE

'I am at perfect liberty to tell you that it would greatly lessen Mr Spode's potentiality for evil, if you were to inform him that you know all about Eulalie, sir.'

Chapter 7, *The Code of the Woosters*

BERTIE SPEAKING TO JEEVES

'The brain. The grey matter. Were you an outstandingly brilliant boy?'
'My mother thought me intelligent, sir.'

'Episode of the Dog McIntosh', *Very Good, Jeeves*

BERTIE SPEAKING TO JEEVES ABOUT MR STOKER

'It is negligible whether Pop Stoker thinks I'm a loony or not. I mean to say, a fellow closely connected by ties of blood with a man who used to walk about on his hands is scarcely in a position, where the question of sanity is concerned, to put on dog and set himself up as an . . .'

'*Arbiter elegentiarum*, sir?'

'Quite. It matters little to me, therefore, from one point of view, what old Stoker thinks about my upper storey. One shrugs the shoulders. But, setting that aside, I admit that this change of heart is welcome. It has come at the right time. I shall accept his invitation. I regard it as . . .'

'The *amende honorable*, sir?'

'I was going to say olive branch.'

'Or olive branch. The two terms are virtually synonymous. The French phrase I would be inclined to consider perhaps slightly the more exact in the circumstances – carrying with it, as it does, the implication of remorse, of the desire to make restitution. But if you prefer the expression "olive branch", by all means employ it, sir.'

'Sinister Behaviour of a Yacht-Owner',
Thank You, Jeeves

BERTIE SPEAKING TO JEEVES

'What was it the poet said of couples like the Bingeese?'

'"Two minds with but a single thought, two hearts that beat as one," sir.'

'A dashed good description, Jeeves.'

'It has, I believe, given uniform satisfaction, sir.'

'Jeeves and the Old School Chum', *Very Good, Jeeves*

JEEVES ADDRESSING BERTIE AND AUNT DAHLIA

'I gather from Mr Seppings, who has had opportunities of overhearing the lady's conversation, that Mrs Trotter, being socially ambitious, is extremely anxious to see Mr Trotter knighted, madam.'

Aunt Dahlia nodded.

'Yes, that's right. She's always talking about it. She thinks it would be one in the eye for Mrs Alderman Blenkinsop.'

'Precisely, madam.'

I was rather surprised.

'Do they knight birds like him?'

'Oh, yes, sir. A gentleman of Mr Trotter's prominence in the world of publishing is always in imminent danger of receiving the accolade.'

Chapter 19, *Jeeves and the Feudal Spirit*

JEEVES SPEAKING TO BERTIE

'I wonder if I have ever happened to mention to you, sir, a Mr Digby Thistleton, with whom I was once in service? Perhaps you have met him? He was a financier. He is now Lord Bridgworth. It was a favourite saying of his that there is always a way.'

'The Artistic Career of Corky', *Carry On, Jeeves*

Jeeves on Jeeves

JEEVES WAS GIVEN THE JOB OF NARRATING JUST ONE STORY, 'BERTIE CHANGES HIS MIND'. THIS EXTRACT FROM ITS FIRST PARAGRAPH REPRESENTS HIS UNDERLYING PHILOSOPHY.

It has happened so frequently in the past few years that young fellows starting in my profession have come to me for a word of advice, that I have found it convenient now to condense my system into a brief formula. 'Resource and Tact' – that is my motto. Tact, of course, has always been with me a *sine qua non*; while as for resource, I think I may say that I have usually contrived to show a certain modicum of what I might call *finesse* in handling those little *contretemps* which inevitably arise from time to time in the daily life of a gentleman's personal gentleman.

'Bertie Changes His Mind', *Carry On, Jeeves*

Editor's Note

It was a great honour to be invited to identify a number of Jeeves's sayings for this collection – especially when I realised that it would involve rereading the eleven novels and thirty-five short stories in which Jeeves played a part.

The range of topics on which Jeeves expressed his views was evidently much broader than one realises when reading one or two of the books. I identified around 200 potential examples, before selecting those which together exemplified the widest range of subject matter.

We will all have different views on which are the funniest – or most deeply philosophical, or just most appropriate – of the quotations I have selected. I hope this little book may encourage you to revisit the stories which include your own favourite comments or exchanges!

Tony Ring
The P G Wodehouse Society (UK)